C334391263

0110100769

ll Lewis:

4/21   BRO,

Books should be returned or renewed by the last
date above. Renew by phone   03000 41 31 31 or
online *www.kent.gov.uk/lies*

Swan Song

GILL LEWIS

Barrington  Stoke

First published in 2021 in Great Britain by
Barrington Stoke Ltd
18 Walker Street, Edinburgh, EH3 7LP

www.barringtonstoke.co.uk

Text © 2021 Gill Lewis
Images © Shutterstock

A CIP catalogue record for this book is available
from the British Library upon request

ISBN: 978-1-78112-954-8

Printed by Hussar Books, Poland

For
the *Nerys-Jane*

I'm waiting for an angel.

My angel.

I even have a long white feather from one of her wings. It's so bright that it seems to glow with its own light.

It sounds a bit crazy, I know. I'm sitting here on the edge of the marsh watching the sky, waiting for her to come back to me. The sky is so big here. This is where the river meets the sea. Beyond the marsh are green fields dotted with sheep, and beyond those are the distant mountains.

I've been watching for days, but this evening there's a cold north wind. It feels as if winter is on its way. The trees are losing their leaves, and the setting sun is turning the sky and the big watery marsh to gold.

It's the perfect evening. I know she'll arrive tonight.

I suppose she's not really an angel. Not in the way people think about angels. But she is one to me.

She changed my life.

She saved me.

It's a long story. But it's true.

It all started a year ago, when I was kicked out of school.

Chapter 1

"Is there anything you'd like to say before you go?" said the head teacher.

We were in his office with Asim, Asim's mother, my mum and me.

I stared at the trophy cabinet behind him full of gold and silver cups. His walls were decorated with pupils' artwork, and on the table was a whole book of newspaper cuttings about all the great things that pupils from the school had done. I didn't fit in there. I wasn't a team player, as I was often told. I was letting the school down. I was letting everyone else down. I was letting myself down. I was a let-down. A failure. A fail.

I didn't want to say anything.

"Dylan," said the head teacher again, "is there anything you want to say to Asim before you go? Do you want to say sorry?"

I looked over at Asim, at his black eye and the stitches above his eyebrow where I'd punched him. Some sticky tape held his broken glasses together.

"No," I mumbled. "He deserved it."

"Well, I think that says it all," said the head teacher as he stood up. "I think we all know what is in everyone's best interests."

Mum sniffed, and I could see she was crying. I felt mad with her for crying. I pushed my chair back, got up and walked to the door. I

saw Asim's mum put her arms around my mum and hug her.

I looked at the head teacher, and he shook his head slowly at me. He didn't say another thing.

I had been expelled.

Permanently excluded.

I turned and walked out of the school and didn't look back.

*

I got in the car and just stared out of the window. It was a grey day. A no-colour day. One of those days so grey, the whole city seems like it's in black and white.

Mum started the car up and pulled away from the school. I wasn't going back there

again. Ever again. I'd got through Year Seven and into Year Eight, and I'd been kicked out before half-term. Maybe I should have been angry or scared, or even happy that it was all over. I should have felt *something*. But in truth, I didn't feel anything at all.

"Well, that's it then," said Mum.

I had nothing to say, and we drove home.

Mum pulled into the drive, and I walked into the house after her. There were boxes and bags in the hallway that hadn't been there before.

"What's going on?" I said.

Mum turned to look at me. "We can't stay here. If I can't work, I can't pay the rent."

I frowned at her. "What are you talking about?"

Mum shook her head. "How can I work if you're not at school?"

"Just go to work," I said. "I'm fine."

"You have no idea, do you?" snapped Mum. "I can't leave you on your own. I have to find a way to make sure you don't miss out on your school work."

"I don't want to do any school work," I shouted. "Don't you get it? I don't want to do anything." I stomped upstairs to my bedroom.

Mum yelled up after me, "Go on then, walk away. But this isn't just about you."

"Shut up!" I yelled. "Just shut up." I slammed my door shut.

I heard Mum storm up the stairs.

She flung the door open. "What's happened to you, Dylan? You worked so hard to get into that grammar school, and now you've just thrown it all away. How has it come to this?"

"Get out," I shouted. I grabbed my Xbox and sat on the bed.

"Fine," said Mum. "Play computer games. Waste your life."

I slammed the door shut behind her. I picked up the Xbox, but I was so angry I threw the console at the wall. It hit with a loud crunch and smashed into tiny bits. I stared at the pieces on the floor. There was no way it could ever be fixed.

I had nothing to do now. Nothing. It was only just past lunch-time, but I lay down on the bed, wrapped my duvet around me and tried to sleep. I had nowhere to go and nothing to do.

I just wanted to sleep and sleep and sleep for ever.

Chapter 2

I slept all the way until the next morning. I woke as it was getting light. I looked at my school bag on the floor. I wouldn't be needing that any more. I sat up and rubbed my eyes.

The house was silent.

I walked downstairs to the kitchen, where everything was in boxes. I put some bread in the toaster and flicked on the TV. The local news told of a couple who had raised money by cycling across Europe and of a fire at a factory. It all felt very far away. I didn't feel part of this world. I spread butter on my toast and

flicked through the channels until I found some cartoons.

"Morning," said Mum, coming downstairs. She switched the kettle on to boil and put a teabag in a mug.

It was strange to see her in her pyjamas. Normally at this time she'd be in her office suit, packing her briefcase, brushing her hair and nagging me to get ready. The firm she worked at was on the other side of the city. But neither of us were going anywhere that day. Both our lives had changed.

I looked at all the boxes packed and taped. "Where are we going?"

"Your grandfather's place," she said.

"Grandad?" I said. "I thought you hated him."

Mum poured boiling water in her mug, sat down and sighed. "I don't hate him. We're just not close. Never have been."

I could only remember going to Grandad's years ago when I was about seven. It wasn't long after Mum and Dad had split up. His house is in Wales near the sea. We were going to stay for a week, but we left after only a day. I remember Mum having an argument with Grandad and getting me quickly back in the car. I didn't really remember Grandad very well at all.

"When are we going?" I said.

"At the weekend," said Mum. "I've got people coming to collect our stuff that has to go into storage. We can only take what we can fit in the car."

"What about school?" I asked.

Mum frowned. "What d'you mean?"

"Well, don't they send someone round to see what I'm doing?" I asked.

"We're on our own now," she said. "I've told the council you're going to be home-schooled."

"But don't they check?" I asked. What if people came round banging on our door to make sure Mum was teaching me?

"No," said Mum. She stirred her tea angrily. "They won't check. You're not their problem any more."

I stared at the TV, but I wasn't really watching. I hadn't thought everything would happen like this. I couldn't really remember how it had all gone wrong. I'd been happy in primary school, really happy. But somehow everything changed at secondary school. I had felt so angry and sad – all mixed up. But people

only saw me angry. I wouldn't let them see me cry.

Mum often had to come and get me from school when I didn't do what the teachers said or messed about in lessons or was rude. Mum blamed it on Dad leaving us. But I don't think it was that. It wasn't like Dad had been around that much anyway. It was as if everything had been building up inside me.

Teachers kept telling us we had to work hard or we'd fail. They said exams were getting more difficult. I was falling behind with work. My friends were changing too, and I couldn't hold on to them – or even to who I was. It was like falling down a deep dark hole that kept getting deeper and deeper and darker and darker. I didn't know when I'd hit the bottom.

And now I wasn't a part of school any more. I wasn't a part of anything. I expect the head

teacher was happy to see to me go, and I didn't know what the other pupils thought of me. It's not like I had any friends any more. Maybe they'd gossip for a day or two but then forget about me. As if I'd never even existed.

I never knew how easy it is for people to vanish.

Chapter 3

The car was packed full. Mum shut the door on our old life, the place where we'd lived since she and Dad split up. Mum had been so busy with work that she hadn't got to know the new neighbours, and there was no one my age in the street. So there was no one to wave us goodbye.

It was just Mum and me.

I don't think anyone saw us go.

I sat with my head propped on pillows and duvets that spilled from the back seat and watched the landscape change from the grey

city streets to flat green fields, until at last we were on the motorway busy with traffic.

Mum hadn't said a word. She just gripped the steering wheel and looked at the cars ahead of us. We were stuck in a traffic jam behind a massive lorry that puffed out black smoke. Just stuck, not going anywhere, with thick black smoke all around us. We couldn't move forwards. We couldn't move backwards. It's how I felt about everything. I closed my eyes and escaped into sleep.

I don't know how long I'd been asleep, but when I woke, the landscape had changed. There were hills rising up on both sides of the road. In the distance were mountains with clouds like dragon's breath clinging to them.

I rubbed my neck and looked over at Mum. Her face had set into a frown. We drove on, through small towns and villages, through woods and up onto mountain roads, until we climbed up to the brim of one hill where Mum pulled into a lay-by.

Below us, a river flowed across a green valley between the hills. The river got wider and wider as it reached the glittering sea. It was late afternoon, and the low October sun was sinking in the west, turning the sea and the river to gold. At the far end of the river, where it opened out into the sea, was a small town, the windows reflecting the setting sun. Smoke drifted from a few of the chimneys. It was so far away from the city. So far away from anywhere. It was a town at the very end of the world.

I looked over at Mum again, but she was staring down at the town, a scowl across her face.

"Is that where Grandad lives?" I asked.

Mum nodded. "I spent so long trying to leave this place," she said, "and now I have to return."

Chapter 4

I didn't know what Grandad would be like.
Mum never talked about him. Maybe he'd be
an angry old man who didn't want us to be
there. Mum must have told him that I'd been
expelled from school, so he'd probably hate me
already.

But Grandad smiled at us when he came to
the door. He stood there in his jeans and an old
chunky jumper that was as white as his hair
and welcomed us in.

"Dylan," he smiled. "Good to see you."

"Hi," I mumbled.

Mum stood in the doorway and didn't go in right away. "Hi, Dad."

Grandad took her coat. "You've had a long journey. Come in, love. I've got a pot of tea on the go."

Grandad lived in a small house on the end of a terrace at the end of the town. It was the last house before the sea. A smell of baking and fresh paint filled the house. He didn't have much furniture inside. He didn't have much at all. He didn't even seem to have a TV. We sat down on the sofa, and Grandad poured tea for himself and Mum and a glass of water for me. He cut a cake into slices for us.

"Spiced apple cake," said Grandad. "Made with apples from the tree."

"You've been painting," said Mum.

Grandad nodded. "I've freshened up your old room and cleared out the attic room for Dylan. Hope they're OK for you."

Mum nodded and ate in silence after that.

Grandad brushed the cake crumbs from his trousers and stood up. "There's a lasagne in the oven for you to heat up tonight. I'm afraid I can't eat with you as I've got choir practice."

"Choir practice?" said Mum. "I didn't know you sang."

Grandad smiled. "I give it a go. I took it up a few years back." He pulled on his cap and headed to the door. "See you later."

Mum went to wash the plates and heat up the lasagne. I looked around the living room. Apart from a bookcase, a sofa and an armchair, the room was bare. There weren't any pictures on the walls, but there was a photo in a silver

frame on the shelf above the fire. I picked it up and looked at it. It was a picture of three people in a small boat.

One of them was Grandad. I knew it was him, but he was a lot younger with dark hair. A woman was standing next to him, her arm linked in his. There was a young girl sitting cross-legged and grinning at the camera. When I looked closely, I could see it was Mum.

I heard Mum coming back into the room, so I shoved the photo back on the shelf, but it fell and the glass smashed on the hard corner of the fire grate.

"What are you doing?" said Mum.

"Nothing," I said. "It fell."

"Dylan!" snapped Mum. She picked up the photo and stared at it.

I peered at the picture too. "Is that you?"

"Yes," she said. She put the photo down and started picking up the bits of glass.

"Is that your mum with you?" I said.

Mum turned to me. "Why don't you go up to your room? I'll call you when supper's ready."

I headed out of the room. I could tell she didn't want to talk about it. But when I looked back, I saw Mum pick up the photo again and stare at it.

It felt odd being in this house where Mum had grown up, not knowing anything about it, or knowing anything about her past.

Chapter 5

The attic room was small with a little window in the roof. Grandad had painted the walls bright white. There was a bed and a chest of drawers and a small table and chair. I could only stand full height right in the middle.
But it was my own space at least. I stood on tiptoes and stared out of the window. It looked towards the sea across fields and marsh. The sun had set, but the sky glowed yellow on the horizon.

After supper, I went to bed with the little window wide open and listened to the wild bird cries. A breeze came in through the window smelling of salt and damp earth. There wasn't the orange glow of city lights I had in my old room. The night was so dark that the stars seemed extra bright. I felt so far away from the house we had left and my school and the city. It really felt as if we were at the very end of the world.

I lay in bed and heard Grandad return, humming as he walked up the street. Mum was in the garden smoking. I don't think they knew I could hear their voices. I lay in bed and listened as their words drifted up with the cigarette smoke through the open window.

"You can stay as long as you want, Gwyn," said Grandad.

"I never wanted to come back," said Mum.

"I know," said Grandad.

I heard Mum sniff.

"I miss Mum," Mum said. "It feels strange being here again."

"I miss her too," said Grandad. He was silent for a moment. "I should have talked to you after she died. I found it too hard to speak about. But I should have tried."

"We both should have talked," agreed Mum. "I couldn't face coming back here. I felt stuck. I just wanted to get away."

"I wish I could turn the clock back and start again," said Grandad. "It's not easy being a parent, is it? I wish I'd known what to do at the time."

"I don't know what to do about Dylan," said Mum.

"Tell me about him," said Grandad. "I'd like to know him better."

I climbed out of bed and tiptoed to the window, wanting and not wanting to hear what she was going to say.

There was a pause before Mum went on. "We used to be really close, him and me. We did everything together. I was proud of him. He was a lovely kid. He was good and kind. Had loads of friends. He worked so hard to get into the grammar school. Then it was like a switch had been flipped. He lost interest in everything. Stopped working. Messed about in class. Swore at teachers and then," she paused again, "he punched a boy."

Grandad was silent.

"He lost all his friends. He's not interested in anything. He'd just sit in his bedroom all day if he could," said Mum. "I lost friends too. People didn't want to know us. The teachers didn't like him. No one did." She talked in a

whisper. "There were times I didn't like him much either. I don't know what's wrong with him."

"When did you last hear him laugh?" said Grandad.

Mum's voice was so quiet. "I don't know," she said. "Maybe it's so long ago, I can't remember."

Grandad sighed. "Give him time, Gwyn."

"How much time?" said Mum.

"As long as it takes," said Grandad. "It sounds like he's depressed. His spirit's broken. He needs time to get better. He needs time to remember how to be himself again."

*

I climbed back into bed. Mum's and Grandad's words swirled inside my head. I tried to think when I had last laughed. Really belly laughed. It had been in the summer between primary and grammar school. Asim and I had been mucking about in the park. We'd kicked our ball into the duck pond, and we'd both gone in after it. But the bottom of the pond was so muddy that we'd fallen in. We'd laughed so much we could hardly stand up again. We were good friends back then, Asim and me.

It was before school started getting serious and before everyone started trying to act cool.

That was the last time I can remember being really happy.

Chapter 6

I woke up when I heard Grandad opening the door to the garage.

I remembered Mum and him talking about me the night before, and it made me feel bad. I didn't want people to talk about me. I wanted to be left alone. I climbed back into bed and pulled the duvet over me, but a few minutes later there was a knock at my door.

"Morning, Dylan," said Grandad. "I'm going out fishing on the boat today if you'd like to come too."

"I'm fine," I mumbled.

"OK," said Grandad. "But if you change your mind, I'm leaving in about twenty minutes."

I lay in bed wanting to sleep, but sleep wouldn't come. What was I going to do all day? I'd broken my Xbox, and Grandad had no TV. Mum had her laptop, but it was rubbish, and I didn't want to ask her to borrow it. Besides, Grandad didn't have any internet connection.

There'd be nothing to do all day. ALL day.

I screwed up my eyes and tried to sleep but felt more awake than ever. I couldn't face being stuck in the house with nothing to do. I couldn't face being stuck in the house with Mum on my case. I got out of bed, pulled my jeans and a top on and went downstairs. "I'll come," I mumbled.

"Excellent," said Grandad.

Mum was sipping tea at the kitchen table. "I'll make some more sandwiches."

Grandad smiled. "We might need a few extra. We'll be back on the evening tide."

"Have you got a phone?" said Mum. I could hear the worry in her question. "Dylan broke his."

"Can't be bothered with them," said Grandad. "I've got a VHF radio in the boat for emergencies."

*

I followed Grandad along the path by the sea wall all the way to the small harbour. The town wasn't one of those picture-postcard tourist places. The houses were small and grey, and the harbour was a dark concrete wall around a small inlet of water.

There were a few people out buying Sunday papers, and they all called good morning to Grandad. I pulled my hood up over my head and kept on walking.

A man on the harbour wall nodded to Grandad. "Morning, Terry. See you've got help today."

"Hello, Evan, this is my grandson, Dylan," said Grandad. "He's come to stay for a bit."

The man nodded. "It's a good day to go out. Weather's set to stay."

I looked out at the boats in the harbour. They were all sitting on the mud, leaning over on their keels.

"We've got about an hour before we can get out on this tide," said Grandad. "I'll go and get some fishing bait. You wait here."

I watched him head off. I didn't want to be left alone and have to talk to people, but Grandad had gone. I walked to the end of the harbour and looked out along the marsh and the estuary, up the river. I sat down and watched the tide creep in across the mud. It was moving fast, swirling in through the harbour, pooling beneath the boats. Two black and white birds with orange beaks and feet ran along the tide line, stabbing into the mud with their long beaks. They flew off and spun away over the harbour wall towards the marsh. I watched them go. There were some people walking along the sea wall and a boy on a mountain bike who cycled in and out between them.

I turned to walk back to the place where Grandad had left me, but the boy on the bike pulled up alongside me. I looked over at him quickly, then did a double take. The boy was a girl.

"You must be Dylan," she said.

She was tall. The bike seemed a bit too
small for her. *How did she know my name?* I
thought. She laughed as if she knew what I was
thinking.

"Everyone knows everyone and everything
here," she laughed. "Fart, and Mrs Lewis in the
post office will know it's you."

I just stared at her.

"I'm Elsie, by the way. Are you going to
come to choir practice with your grandad?"

I shrugged. I couldn't think of anything to
say. I didn't really want her to know anything
else about me.

Elsie pushed off on her bike. "See you
around," she said. And then she was gone,
pedalling along the harbour wall.

The tide had crept into the harbour by the time Grandad got back, and the boats near the harbour entrance were already afloat. Another man carrying a fishing rod was walking close behind Grandad. He stopped and stared at us.

"Morning, Alan," said Grandad.

Alan looked over at me. "Don't want no trouble here, lad," he said. "I hear you were expelled from your last school."

Grandad started packing things into a small wooden rowing boat. "Leave it, Alan," he said. "Nothing to do with you."

"We'll know where to look if anything in town gets vandalised," Alan said.

I pulled my hood up even higher. Elsie was right – everyone here knew all about me.

Grandad ignored Alan and climbed into the rowing boat. "Hop in, Dylan," he said.

I sat opposite Grandad as he rowed across the harbour. "That one's ours," he said. He pointed to a small blue motorboat that had a closed cabin and an open deck. It was named the *Nerys-Jane*. He pulled things onto her deck and tied the rowing boat up next to her.

"Everything has to have a place in a boat," said Grandad as he put the fish bait in a bucket by the rest of his fishing gear. He filled up the engine with fuel and handed me a life jacket.

"I'm OK," I mumbled.

"No choice," said Grandad. "You have to wear it."

I looked up. There wasn't a cloud in the sky, and there was no wind at all.

"It's shallow where the river meets the sea," said Grandad. "The waves that roll in from the ocean can get big there at times."

I pulled the life jacket on, and Grandad handed me the box with our lunch. "Go and put this in the cabin," he said.

I ducked my head and went down into the small cosy cabin. There were two seats along the sides, which looked like they could be used for sleeping, and a table in the middle. I put the food under one of the benches, and by the time I got back up on deck, Grandad had started up the engine and was steering out of the harbour into the estuary, towards the wide open sea.

Chapter 7

I sat on the deck and watched as Grandad steered out along the river channel between the sandbanks.

I saw two of the black and white birds I'd seen before with the orange beaks and feet.

"They're oystercatchers," said Grandad. He then pointed to a brown bird with long red legs and a long beak it was poking in the mud. "And that's a redshank."

I just sat and watched the marsh and fields pass by as we headed out towards the sea. The

thrum of the engine and the wheeling gulls calling above us were the only sounds.

As we neared the opening to the sea, Grandad slowed the boat and stood up, his hand over his eyes to shade against the sun. "It's fine today," he said. "The waves aren't that big." He pointed out to sea. "You see the swell rises and gets bigger here. It's because there's a sandbar – a ridge of sand beneath the sea. It can be tricky getting out and in."

Grandad waited for a lull in the bigger waves and then steered out into the sea. The little boat rose and dipped over the waves rolling in from the Atlantic, and then we were out in calmer water.

"There's a little cove we'll anchor in," said Grandad. He pointed to the ship's wheel. "Here, you have a go at steering," he said, standing back from the wheel.

"Grandad!" I said. "I don't know what to do!"

"Have a go," Grandad laughed. "This is the throttle. Push it forwards to go faster. Backwards to slow down and into this position for neutral." He pointed to a headland. "We want to go to a small bay on the other side of that."

And with that he went down into the cabin, stretched out on the bench and closed his eyes.

"Grandad!" I said. "I can't drive a boat!"

Grandad opened one eye. "Wake me when we get there."

I held on to the ship's wheel and stared ahead, almost too scared to move. I turned the wheel towards the headland, and the boat swung too much the other way. When I turned the wheel again, it lurched back too far. I

thought Grandad would shout at me, but his eyes were still closed.

I tried again and got the hang of steering. Then I tried to push the throttle forwards and the nose of the boat lifted a little out of the water. A white frothy wake trailed behind us.

I was concentrating so hard on steering that I didn't notice something rise up beside the boat, a sleek curve that leapt beside me. Another one leapt out of the water, spinning in the air before it crashed back into the water.

"Dolphins!" I yelled. "Grandad! Dolphins!"

Grandad was up like a shot. He took the wheel so that I could watch them. One looked me right in the eye, and I had the feeling it wanted to know about me just as much as I wanted to know about it. I couldn't believe I was seeing real dolphins.

"We're lucky," said Grandad. "The bottlenose dolphins can be a bit shy."

Grandad steered us to the other side of the headland, where he dropped an anchor in the calm water. He put bait on the hook of his fishing rod and cast the line out into the sea. Then he poured himself a cup of coffee, passed a cola to me and sat back.

"What do we do now?" I asked.

Grandad looked at me. "We eat and sit," he said. "Or have a little snooze. Or a think. Up to you. I'm going to read my book."

"OK," I said. I never sat and did nothing without the TV on or my Xbox to play with. I took my sandwiches, walked to the front of the deck and sat down with my legs over the side. I lay back and looked up at the sky. I took a deep breath in and out. In and out. It was such

a big sky. I hadn't ever looked at the sky back at school. I hadn't looked at the sky for a long, long time.

I must have fallen asleep, because when I woke, a chill wind was blowing and I had goosebumps on my arms. Grandad had put away his fishing gear and started up the engine.

"We'd better head back," said Grandad. "The wind's picked up. The tide has turned again and will help us in."

"We haven't caught any fish," I said.

Grandad smiled. "Maybe another day. It's not about the fish. I just like to get out on the water."

I sat next to Grandad as the *Nerys-Jane* rose and dipped over the swell. When we reached the sandbar again, the waves were higher than before, and I could see some of them were breaking as they entered the estuary.

"Hold on," said Grandad. "Just in case. We have to choose a wave and follow close behind it on the way in. Just let me know if another wave behind is catching up."

Grandad waited until he had chosen a wave to follow, then he pushed the boat to full speed, and we raced in just behind the wave. I looked back to see another wave chasing us in. It was bigger than our wave, and it broke into surf, but Grandad kept ahead of it and steered us safely in.

"Here," said Grandad when we were in calm water. "Why don't you take over now?"

The estuary looked different. All the sandbanks were covered by the tide, and the

river was wide, reaching right across the marsh. The sun was lower in the sky, and a few clouds were over the mountains. The breeze was colder than before.

"A northerly wind," said Grandad, nodding.

"Are we going into the harbour?" I asked.

Grandad looked up at the sky again. "No. Let's go a bit further up-river. I think it'll happen this evening."

"What?" I said.

Grandad turned to me and smiled. "The greatest show on earth."

Chapter 8

I steered the boat past the harbour, then Grandad switched off the engine, and we drifted up-river with the incoming tide. We passed Grandad's house and carried on until we were next to green fields. Grandad dropped the anchor, and the boat tugged at the rope while the sea flowed in past us.

"That's Maggie Williams' farm," said Grandad, pointing to farm buildings further up the hill. The hedgerows were overgrown, and the farm buildings looked empty and shabby. "She died last year. Her land goes all the way

over the hill and down to the marsh here. Her son lives in London and wants to sell up."

It was getting colder now, and Grandad saw I was shivering. He went into the cabin to get a blanket and wrapped it around me.

"Look to the northern sky," he said, pointing beyond the mountains. "Look! Here they come. The north wind is bringing them home."

High above, the sky was deep blue. It was such a deep colour that a few stars had begun to twinkle. The thin clouds were rimmed with gold from the rays of the setting sun.

Then I saw them.

There was a line of birds in the distance shaped in a V. I could see about twenty birds against the sky, and as they drew nearer I saw their long necks outstretched and their wings

beating. One bird led the point of the V, and the others followed.

"Whooper swans," Grandad whispered. "All the way from Iceland."

"Iceland?" I said.

Grandad nodded. "The winter is milder here. They stay here all winter and then fly back to Iceland in March to breed."

The swans arrived quickly, filling up the sky with their honking calls and the creak and swish of their wing beats. Their white feathers gleamed gold in the sun as they flew in a low circle above the estuary, then came down right over the *Nerys-Jane*. Right over Grandad and me. They were so low I could see their feet tucked up underneath them. Then they came in to land on the marsh beside the green fields, back-beating their wings and putting their

feet out to slide along the water. They were big white swans with yellow beaks tipped with black.

They waddled onto the green fields, flapping and honking at each other before bending their necks to feed on the grass.

"They return every year to this estuary, to Maggie Williams' fields by the marsh. Locals call them the Swan Fields," said Grandad. "The swans bring the winter with them."

We watched the swans for a while. Grandad was looking through binoculars and writing numbers in a small book.

"I write down their leg ring numbers," he said. "Then the scientists can work out which birds return."

As the sun sank even lower, it became difficult to see, so Grandad started the engine, pulled up the anchor and we steered back to the harbour.

It was strange to put my feet on solid land again. I felt heavy. Stuck back in the old me. I pulled my hood up over my head and stared out at the *Nerys-Jane* bobbing in the harbour. All I could think was that I wanted to get back out on the water where there was no talk of school, no school bells or homework. No tests or timetables. No walls or corridors.

Just the wind, the waves and the wild white swans.

A place where the world was turning.

A place where, for the first time in a long while, I had felt free.

Chapter 9

Mum was cooking dinner when we got home, the smell of roasting potatoes drifting down the road to greet us. Grandad lit the fire. It was a real fire with real logs and real flames. My face felt reddened from the sun and wind even though it was late October, and my hair felt sticky with salt spray. I curled up on the armchair by the fire, and Grandad passed me a book that was open at a page with the picture of a whooper swan.

"There you go," said Grandad. "That's what we saw today."

He left the room, and I read about the swans. I flicked over other pages, seeing pictures of the oystercatchers and redshanks we'd seen too.

He came back in to say supper was ready and pointed to a bookcase in the corner. "Help yourself to any books you want to read," he said.

We all ate supper in silence, but it was a nice silence, not like the silences between Mum and me when we'd had an argument and couldn't agree. I wanted to ask Grandad when he was going out on the boat again, but I didn't want to seem too keen.

Grandad must have been thinking the same thing, because he looked out at the dark sky. "There's wet and windy weather for the rest of the week. Too windy to get out on the boat."

He must have known I felt sad about that. "Well, you can borrow my bike anytime," he went on. "It's a bit of a boneshaker, I'm afraid."

"Where do I go?" I asked.

Grandad looked at me. "What do you mean?"

"Where am I allowed to go?"

Grandad shrugged. "Go where you like. Explore. Why do you need me to tell you where to go?"

"OK," I said. I frowned. In my old life, I was always told where to go and when to be somewhere. It felt odd to be free to do my own thing.

Grandad got up and stacked the empty plates. "Thanks, Gwyn, that was delicious."

"Thanks, Mum," I mumbled.

Mum looked surprised, but she didn't say anything. I don't think I had said thank you to her for a long, long time.

As there was no TV in Grandad's house, I crouched down and looked at the bookcase. There were more bird books, books about Wales, crime novels and boating magazines. I pulled out one book with a title I knew: *The Hobbit*. I'd seen the film. There was nothing else to do. Maybe I would read the book.

I went upstairs to my room. Rain was pattering on the window. It was cold in the attic, and so I curled up under the duvet and began to read. And while a storm picked up outside, I was soon in another world where there were hobbits and wizards, and they were setting out on a quest to fight a dragon.

Chapter 10

It rained all through the next morning. It pattered on the roof. When I looked out, the rain was so thick that I couldn't see the estuary. I stayed in bed and read and read. I read *The Hobbit* all the way to the end, and then suddenly it was lunch-time.

Mum and Grandad were out of the house, and there was a note to say to help myself to soup and toast. I sat down to eat and noticed Mum had left a pile of books about home education. I didn't want to hear her talk about it when she got back, so I finished my lunch, grabbed a raincoat and went to look for Grandad's bike.

It was an old bike. Three gears and an old leather saddle. I put his cycle helmet on and pushed the bike out onto the road. *Which way should I go?* I thought. It was weird not being told what to do, when to do it and where to go. It was even weirder going outside on a school day. I felt as if I was doing something wrong, like a police officer might come along and tell me off.

I sat on the saddle and pushed off, heading away from the town. I cycled up the hill and found a place where I could see the whole coast. The rain had stopped, and the sky was clear out over the sea. I could see the estuary and the small cove that we had anchored in the day before. I headed down over the other side of the hill and then around the coast road back to the town. Now the roads were busy

with traffic, and there were students in school uniform walking along the pavement. I didn't want to be seen, so I turned my bike off onto a track that ran alongside the Swan Fields.

I stopped to look at the swans. There were more than the day before. They must have arrived in the night or in the morning. It was strange to think they had flown all the way from Iceland over icecaps, mountains and seas. I climbed onto the wall and sat and watched them. One swan was sitting apart from the rest. It had its head tucked under its wing.

"Hello again."

I turned to see that Elsie had pulled up beside me on her bike.

"What you doing?" she said.

I shrugged. "Nothing."

"Are you watching the swans like your grandad?"

I nodded.

"Everyone calls him the Swan Man, didn't you know?"

I shook my head and looked back out at the swans. The flock had moved further up the field, but the swan on its own couldn't stand. It took a few steps but fell to the ground, its long neck stretched out.

Elsie saw it too.

"There's something wrong with it," I said.

"Come on," she said. "Let's go and take a look."

"Is it safe?" I said. "I heard swans can break your arm."

Elsie laughed and hopped over the fence. "You don't believe that, do you?"

I followed her to the swan. It saw us and tried to flap away, but it couldn't move far.

Elsie took off her jacket and wrapped it around the swan's wings. "You support its head," she said.

Between us, we carried the swan back along the road to Grandad's house. Back to Grandad, the Swan Man. It was heavy, and I'd never seen a bird so close up. Its small black eyes watched me all the way home.

*

Grandad led us into the kitchen and put the swan on the table. He ran his fingers all over it.

"It's got fishing line wrapped around its neck," he said. "I don't think it's been able to

swallow properly for a long time. It's very thin.
I'm surprised it's still alive."

Grandad went to find his old notebook. He
read the swan's tag and looked it up in his
lists and notes. "This one's a female. She was
ringed in a field seven years ago in a place
called Skagafjördur in north-west Iceland."

"What shall we do?" I asked.

"We'll take her to the vet," said Grandad.
"Let's hope the vet can help her."

Mum drove us all to the vet's surgery. We
had to wait for a while, but then the vet called
us in. She examined our swan and cut away
the fishing line caught around her neck. Then
she did an X-ray to make sure there wasn't a
fishing hook or lead fishing weights inside her.

"She's lucky," said the vet. "But she hasn't been able to eat with that fishing line around her neck. She needs feeding up."

"We can do that," said Grandad. "I've got an old chicken pen outside. If she's with us, then she's within sight and sound of the other swans on the Swan Fields. The Swan Study Group can give us advice."

The vet nodded. "Sounds like a good plan."

Back at Grandad's house, Elsie and I helped him get the chicken pen ready. We put straw down on the ground and a bowl of water.

Grandad built a wooden shelter for the swan. "Birds make an oil from a gland at the base of their tail," he said. "They spread it over their feathers to waterproof them. If they're ill, they can't do this so well and can get wet and cold."

I held out some grain that Grandad
had bought and offered it to the swan. She
stretched her neck forward and then began
guzzling from my hand. I giggled as her beak
tickled my palm.

"She's hungry and wants to eat," laughed
Grandad. "That's good to see."

Elsie and I fed her some more, and then
Grandad said we should let her rest.

"Can I come back and see her?" asked Elsie.

"Of course," said Grandad.

*

I went with Elsie to fetch our bikes from where
we'd left them by the Swan Fields.

Elsie turned to me. "Come to choir practice tomorrow." She pushed her bike to the road. "It'll be more fun. Everyone else is ancient."

"Why do you go?" I asked.

"I have to. Dad runs it. He's the choirmaster," said Elsie.

I shrugged.

"Please come," said Elsie.

I cycled home and went to put some more grain down for the swan. It was twilight, and she had already put her head under her wing to sleep. I picked up a long white flight feather that had fallen to the ground. It was strange to think this feather had helped to carry her thousands of miles.

I closed the door of the pen so that she'd be safe from foxes in the night.

I knew she needed me.

I had helped her survive.

What I didn't know then is how much I would need her too.

Chapter 11

The town hall was cold, and most people had kept their coats on.

Elsie grinned when I walked in. "You came then!"

I went to sit beside her. She had been right. Most people in the choir were really old – at least over fifty.

"I expect we'll be in the same part of the choir," said Elsie, looking at me. "Your voice hasn't broken yet."

I suddenly felt embarrassed. I hadn't sung since primary school. "I'm no good at singing," I said.

Elsie laughed. "That's what everyone says."

Elsie's dad had us all doing breathing and singing exercises to warm up. We had to make all sorts of silly sounds, and I started laughing after we had to make weird alien noises through our noses. I thought we'd sing hymns and boring stuff, but we sang lots of songs I knew and some ones for Christmas too.

One old lady sang a solo part. Her voice was thin and so quiet it was hard to hear her, and she was definitely out of tune.

"Couldn't your dad choose someone else for the solo?" I whispered.

Elsie gave me a funny look. "Dad says it's not about being the best. He makes sure

everyone gets to sing solo if they want to. You should try it."

I didn't like the thought of that. "Not me," I said.

The session went by so fast that I was a bit sad it was over so soon.

There was coffee and hot chocolate and cake afterwards. People came up and chatted to me. That never happened in my old life. I met some of Grandad's friends. One was Jim. He'd been a Science teacher, but he'd retired and now he helped out as a crew member for the local lifeboat. His wife, Kate, had been an English teacher. I thought they'd ask me about school, but instead Jim chatted about the estuary and some of the rescues he had been on. Kate asked me about what books I liked, and we got talking about *The Hobbit* and *The Lord of the Rings*.

Grandad and I walked home through the rain after that. He hummed some of the tunes, and I joined in.

When we got home, Mum was sitting by the fire reading a book.

"You should come with us next time, Gwyn," said Grandad. "People were asking after you."

Mum shrugged. "It's a bit awkward. People might remember me as the girl who wanted to get away from here."

Grandad sat down beside her. "People understand. Also, Elsie's dad asked if you'd have a look at his tax return. He's a bit stuck."

Mum nodded. "Not doing much else, am I?"

I went to bed after that, but before I curled up under the duvet, I opened the window and listened to the rain and the wind coming in

from the sea. It was a different sort of song, a song of the wild. I watched huge clouds move like ships across the sky, sometimes blotting out the moon.

As I drifted into sleep, I thought about the swans settled down on the marsh, where they roosted together at night. I thought of them with their heads tucked beneath their warm feathers so as to sleep safely through the worst of the weather. I thought of the swan we'd rescued and hoped we'd be able to set her free to sing her wild song again too.

Chapter 12

Christmas and New Year came and went in a warm glow of choir practice and carol services. We sang at the old people's home; we sang in the harbour, raising money for the lifeboats; we sang in the church; and we sang in the town hall on New Year's Eve. Even Mum joined us as we all sang in the new year.

I looked after our swan all the time: I fed her, cleaned her pen and just sat with her. Sometimes I even took a book into the pen to read aloud to her. I think she liked it, because she always came and sat beside me, eating

from my hand, then stretching her wings and waggling her tail before she settled down.

In the first week of January, the Swan Study Group told Grandad that it was time for our swan to go back to the wild. I was sad and happy at the same time. Happy that we'd saved her, but sad that I wouldn't have her to look after. I'd miss her.

We went as a small group – Grandad, Mum, Elsie and me. We took her to the Swan Fields, and we let her go. She shook herself and waddled over to the others, where they honked to each other, but then she started to feed on the grasses with them as if she'd never been anywhere else.

I think Grandad knew how I was feeling, because he patted me on the back. "Well done, Dylan. She'll live to fly back to Iceland again because of you. You saved a life."

"We did it together," I said.

Grandad nodded. "Come on. Let's get home. There's cake in the oven."

Rain had started to fall, and I pulled up my hood against the sharp wind. My old life in the city seemed so long ago. I hadn't done any school work at all since I'd come to Grandad's, and Mum hadn't said anything. I had read books though – loads of books. I'd forgotten how much I'd loved reading. The librarian in town had got to know me well. She always had new ideas for what to read next each time I went.

Mum seemed happier too. Some of Grandad's other friends had asked her to help them with tax returns and business stuff, and she said she liked being busy and useful. She'd got Grandad to agree to connect to the internet so that she could work at home.

Grandad and I even went out on the *Nerys-Jane*. One cold February day, when the sky was pale blue and there were no clouds, we took her out onto the estuary. The air was so still that the water was like a mirror. The light was so bright that you could see everything – even the mountains looked so close that you could almost touch them.

We motored up-river, and Grandad slowed down as we passed the Swan Fields. I grabbed his binoculars and scanned the field, trying to see the numbers on the leg rings.

"There's our swan," I called. "Second from the right."

Grandad took back the binoculars and looked through them too.

Our swan stood up tall and looked over at us. I couldn't help waving to her. Grandad steered the boat further up the river, and then I saw our swan waddle towards us. She began beating her wings and running with her feet flapping beneath her until she took off into the air. She kept flying until she was level with the *Nerys-Jane*, and then she flew alongside us. I felt she was looking at me all the time.

"Does she know who I am?" I asked Grandad.

"I'm sure she does," said Grandad. "Birds are very intelligent. They know people by their faces."

Grandad slowed the boat to a stop and our swan came in to land on the water, feet outstretched and sliding across the surface. She waggled her tail and swam up to the boat. I pulled the crust off my sandwich and threw it to her. She followed us for the whole trip, only returning to the Swan Fields as we headed back to the harbour.

On the way back, we could see a sign at the track up to Maggie Williams' farm.

Grandad looked through the binoculars. "It's up for sale."

"Who'll buy it?" I asked.

Grandad shrugged. "Not much money in farming these days."

I stared at the farm as we drifted by. Grandad said it had been in the same family for over three hundred years. He also said swans have been using this area for many thousands of years. It made me think how strange it is that people think they can claim a piece of land for their own and do what they want with it.

When we got back to the cottage, Grandad's friend Jim was waiting for us.

Mum had cake and a pot of coffee on the go. "I asked Jim to see if he could give you some lessons," said Mum.

I frowned. "School lessons?"

Jim smiled. "Your mum thought you might want me to teach you some Science and Maths."

"What about English and other subjects?" I said.

"You read a lot, don't you?" said Jim.

I nodded.

"That'll do for now, but it might be good to keep up with Maths and Science," said Jim.

I shrugged. I didn't want to think about school. I liked things how they were.

"Just have one lesson," said Jim. "If you don't like it, I can go."

I sat down with him at the kitchen table. I expected him to go back over times tables and word problems and shapes, but instead he brought out a map of the estuary for boats. He talked a bit about his job as a member of the lifeboat crew and then showed me how to work out the depths of the estuary at different places at different heights of the tide. Then he got me to work out how to take a bearing and work out how fast a boat would go and how the tides worked. Each time he asked me to work something out, Jim told me a different story of a rescue at sea.

"Maths saves lives," he said at last as he folded the map away.

I just stared at the map in his hands. "I've missed a lot of school work," I said. "I'll never catch up."

"Rubbish," said Jim. "There's plenty of time. We just need to get you enjoying it again."

When Jim had left, Mum turned to me. "Well?" she said. "What did you think?"

I shrugged. I didn't want to seem too keen. But the truth was I wanted to have another lesson with Jim. There was so much I didn't know. And I began to want to find out more.

Chapter 13

As winter turned into spring, Grandad and I spent more time out on the estuary. Our swan always flew close beside us on our trips, keeping us company. Grandad let me steer the boat, and he taught me lots of sailor's knots, how to look after the engine and how to use the VHF radio. As the days got longer, the sun's arc rose higher each day.

Grandad pointed to the swans feeding on the fields. "Won't be long before they leave," he said.

I stared out at the swans. "Will we have to wait until next autumn before they come back?"

Grandad nodded. "But we get other amazing birds in the summer. Wait till you see the ospreys. We've had several catching fish from this estuary."

Lessons with Jim were going well too. They didn't really feel like lessons. For a few sessions he focused on the swans. He said he didn't know much about them, so we found out about them together: about what they looked like inside, and how they flew, and how they could fly so high. We both came up with a list of questions and tried to find the answers.

But one day, Jim came into the cottage with a frown on his face.

"What's up?" asked Grandad.

"It's Maggie Williams' farm," said Jim grimly. "Alan Jenkins wants to buy the Swan Fields."

Grandad frowned. "He's a nasty piece of work. What does Alan Jenkins want the Swan Fields for?"

"He wants to turn them into a holiday park," said Jim. "Caravans and a swimming-pool complex."

"He can't do that," said Grandad.

"He's on the council," said Jim. "He'll get it passed. Somehow he always gets his way."

Jim didn't feel like doing any Science or Maths after that, and neither did I. He left early. I went to find Grandad, but Mum said he'd already gone to bed. I went up to my bedroom too and looked out of the window. The fields and marsh were cloaked in soft blue darkness. I could hear the calls of the swans from the marsh as they settled to roost. Their song was different somehow. Sadder. I didn't want to think about bright lights and noise from a holiday park instead of the Swan Fields.

The next morning, I was up early with Grandad to catch the tide out onto the estuary. A pink dawn spread across the sky. Grandad didn't say much. He seemed worried too. He even forgot to pack some sandwiches, so I grabbed some bread and cheese and made a Thermos of coffee.

Grandad started up the engine of the *Nerys-Jane*, and we motored out onto a cold flat sea.

"Wind's picking up this afternoon," Grandad said. "We won't stay out long."

We went up-river at first, but even before we got to the Swan Fields I knew something felt different. There were no honking calls of swans feeding on the grasses. The fields were empty.

Part of me hoped our swan would have stayed, but there were none to be seen. I looked north, hoping to see a distant V of birds in flight. But the swans had gone. It was a big wide empty sky.

I tried to think about our swan beating her wings high above the clouds. Maybe she was already over the sea by now, heading to Iceland.

"We'll be here when they return," I said to Grandad.

"But their fields won't be," said Grandad. He looked so angry. I'd never seen him so angry before. "They won't have the fields to come

back to. Alan Jenkins will say the holiday park
is good for tourism and makes money for the
town, and he'll get it passed through. Then the
fields will be gone. The swans will be gone too."
Grandad stopped and put his head in his hands
and started crying. He sobbed and sobbed. The
boat was drifting towards the marsh, so I took
the wheel and steered her down-river towards
the open sea.

Grandad came to stand beside me after a
while. "I'm sorry," he said.

"I'm sorry about the Swan Fields too," I said.

"Your grandmother loved the swans,"
said Grandad. "But she died. Back then, men
weren't meant to show feelings, so I hid them
from your mother. I just closed up. I never
talked about your grandmother. She was my
wife. My Eve. My whole world stopped when

she died. It was the swans that saved me. They showed me the world was still turning."

I let Grandad take us over the sandbar and on out to sea. The wind was fresh and whipped up small white peaks. Grandad anchored in our cove and said he needed a rest in the cabin. He said he had a headache from all the stress of finding out about the Swan Fields.

I put a rod out with bait and ate my sandwiches while Grandad rested. I looked over at him once or twice, but he was fast asleep.

The wind seemed to be picking up some more. The waves crested and curled, and the *Nerys-Jane* tugged at her anchor rope. Far away on the horizon, the sky seemed heavy and black. Storm clouds were coming, and I remembered Jim telling me how strong the winds under a thunder cloud can be.

I reeled in the fishing line, and as I did so I heard a honking call in the sky above me. It was my swan flying in a circle above the boat. She hadn't left with the other swans after all. She was still here. I threw a crust from my sandwich, but she didn't want to land in the water. Maybe it was too rough for her. She was trying to tell me something. I felt a pit of worry deep inside.

"Grandad," I called. "I think there's a storm coming. We'd better get back."

But Grandad didn't answer.

I went down into the cabin.

"Grandad?" I said.

Grandad grunted something, but his words were strange and slurred. He tried to get up, but he fell down into the gap between the two benches.

The waves were getting bigger, rocking the boat from side to side.

"Grandad!" I said again.

A big wave thumped against the boat and sent me falling on top of him. I got up quickly up and tried pull Grandad up too, but he couldn't move. He tried to talk, but no words came out.

"Grandad!" I yelled again. But he couldn't answer. Grandad was really ill, and we were out alone on a rough and stormy sea.

Chapter 14

The swan called again, and when I looked out of the cabin she was flying in circles above the *Nerys-Jane*. It was as if she wanted me to get going.

"Come on, Dylan," I yelled into the wind. "Do something."

I did everything I could remember. I started the engine and pulled the anchor up. The *Nerys-Jane* pitched and rolled until I pushed her forwards through the waves. I switched on the VHF radio, remembering the channel Grandad said to use in emergencies. Someone answered my call. I told them my

position and that Grandad was ill and I was bringing him back to the harbour.

My hands were shaking all the time and my legs felt like jelly.

The dark storm cloud was getting closer and closer, and the blue-green water had turned black and churned with big waves.

I steered towards the entrance to the estuary. Waves were rolling and breaking over the sandbar. I remember Grandad saying I had to choose a wave and ride behind it on the way in, otherwise the boat would turn over.

But which wave? They were all falling into each other. Then I heard my swan. I looked up to see her against a ray of sunlight that had broken through the dark cloud. Her feathers looked like they had gold edges in the last of the sun. She looked like an angel. My angel.

She circled once and then headed towards the estuary for me to follow. I pushed the *Nerys-Jane* full throttle behind a wave. I kept the boat right behind it; the foam from its crest was flying back against us. I turned to see a larger wave behind. It curled and broke and chased us in, a foaming wall of surf. It was faster than us, outrunning us. It foamed around the *Nerys-Jane* and lifted her up, turning her on her side. The propellers spun in air, and I thought we were going to flip over. I saw my swan ahead, flying low over the waves, leading the way. Another wave knocked us the right way, and I pushed the engine full speed ahead. We shot forwards with the wave, the sea boiling around us. All the time I kept my eyes fixed on my swan, my angel, guiding us in.

Even when we passed the sandbar, I still kept my eyes fixed on my swan, so I didn't notice an orange lifeboat speeding towards me. It was Jim and the lifeboat crew. They drew

alongside, and Jim and another crew member came aboard.

They went down to look at Grandad.

"How is he?" I asked.

"He's OK for now," said Jim. "There's an ambulance waiting at the harbour. Best get there as soon as we can."

Jim took over the boat; I sat next to him and couldn't stop shaking.

"That was impressive," said Jim. "I saw you bring the boat in over the sandbar. That's very brave. Not many proper sailors could do that. Maybe you'll be on our lifeboat crew one day."

I shook my head. "I couldn't be. I was so scared."

Jim turned to look at me. "I've been scared before too," he said. "Being brave is knowing you're scared but going anyway."

As we got near the harbour, I looked out for my angel. I needed her. I needed her to tell me Grandad would be OK. She had warned me and helped me. She had saved me. But there were no swans on the swan fields. All I could see was one swan on its own, high, high above us, heading towards the northern sky.

She had already left.

I knew my angel had gone.

Chapter 15

The first thing I saw on the harbour wall were the blue flashing lights of the ambulance, and then I saw Mum too.

Jim said he'd take care of the *Nerys-Jane*. The paramedics put Grandad on a stretcher and carried him into the ambulance. Mum and I drove behind them to the hospital in the car.

By the time we got to see him, Grandad was in a bed on a ward. The doctor told us that Grandad had had a stroke. He said it was something that sometimes happened in older people, where a blood clot stops blood getting to parts of the brain. The doctor warned us that Grandad might not walk or talk again. But he said he had the best chance of getting better because I got him to the hospital so quickly.

I sat in silence on the way home. In just one day, everything had changed. The swans had gone, Grandad was in hospital, and the cottage seemed empty without him.

Jim and his wife, Kate, brought a stew and cooked it for us.

"It was the stress of hearing about the Swan Fields going up for sale that did it," Mum said.

I felt so angry. And I couldn't do anything to help. "I can't make Grandad better, and I can't stop Alan Jenkins from buying the Swan Fields," I said.

Kate leaned forward. "There is a saying: you have to learn to accept the things you

cannot change, but be brave enough to change the things you can."

"What do you mean?" I asked.

Kate smiled. "Only the doctors and time can help your grandad get better. But maybe there is a way to stop Alan Jenkins."

"How?" I asked.

Kate shook her head. "That's what we have to work out."

Chapter 16

Grandad did improve. Slowly. The doctors said he was lucky. He began to learn to walk again with the help of a frame. But he still couldn't talk. His words were slurred. He seemed to get better on the outside, but he didn't want to see people any more, not even his friends in the choir.

April passed into May and then into June, and at the end of June he came home. Mum put his bed in the downstairs room and arranged for a stairlift to be fitted. She tried to help Grandad to type what he wanted to say on

her laptop. But he didn't seem to want to say anything at all.

But one day, Grandad typed a question I didn't want to answer:

When are the Swan Fields being sold?

"At the end of July, Jim says," I answered.

Grandad got really cross. He tried to say something, but the words slurred and he became even more angry.

Lost everything, he typed. **My wife, my boat, my voice, my choir, my swans**.

"I'll take you out on the boat one day, Grandad," I said. "Jim said he'd help us."

But Grandad just turned away from me. When I left, I heard him throwing stuff about the room and the sound of ripping paper. I went to my room and curled up on my bed because I didn't know what else to do.

*

The next day, Mum took Grandad to hospital for a check-up. I was reading in the garden when Elsie turned up.

"Shouldn't you be at school?" I said.

She laughed. "We've broken up for summer, silly."

"Oh," I said.

"How's your grandad?" she asked. "We miss him at the choir."

"He's not right," I said. "He was ripping stuff up last night."

"What sort of stuff?"

I took her into Grandad's room. There was paper everywhere. I pulled his swan notebook out of the bin. He'd thrown away the record of all the ring numbers and sightings that he'd made over the years.

Elsie pulled out a piece of paper, flattened it and read it.

She stared at it for a long time.

"What is it?" I asked.

"It's a poem," she said. "Who's Eve?"

"My grandma," I said. "Grandad's wife. I never knew her."

"It's a love song to her," said Elsie.

I pulled a face. "Yuk."

"It's beautiful," said Elsie. "It's called 'Swan Song' and it says it's for Eve. You must read it."

I read the song. Elsie was right – it was beautiful. And then I understood why the swans were so important to Grandad. They connected him to her, to Eve. When the swans came back, it was as if a bit of Eve came back with them too.

Swan Song
For Eve

When the cold north wind is blowing
And storms rage across the sea
I stand and call your name
And I call you back to me.

Come back home, come back home
Come back home to me.

Your home is in this valley
In this salt marsh estuary
Here beneath this winter sky
You belong with me.

Come back home, come back home
Come back home to me.

I see white wings over water
And I see you flying free
I want to hold you one more time
I want you here with me.

Come back home, come back home
Come back home to me.

And when the dark is falling
And I can no longer see
I feel your wings around me
And know you're here with me.

Come back home, come back home
Come back home to me.

Chapter 17

Elsie pulled out her phone and took a photo of Grandad's song.

"What are you doing?" I said.

"Dad can put music to it," said Elsie. "The choir could sing it to him."

"Maybe Grandad doesn't want us to read it. It's personal, isn't it?" I said. "It's not like it'll stop the Swan Fields being sold."

"We could sing it in the Town Hall," said Elsie. "Let people know we want to save the

Swan Fields. Maybe they will want to save them too."

I just stared at her. "That's it," I said. "Why don't we see if we can get people to raise money to buy the fields?"

"How?" said Elsie.

"A crowdfunder," I said. "People do it all the time. We could record the song and tell Grandad's story."

"We'd have to raise a lot of money," said Elsie. "And no one's got much to spare."

"It's worth a try," I said. I remembered Kate's words: *be brave enough to change the things you can.* "It's definitely worth a try."

*

And so Elsie's dad put Grandad's words to music. The choir practised it, and Jim took me out on his boat and we used his camera to take some photos and videos of the estuary to tell Grandad's story. Then we recorded the song, and Mum helped me set up a crowdfunding page.

Grandad was cross with me at first that I had read his song, but when he heard that we were trying to use it to help us buy the fields, he became interested. Mum pushed him in a wheelchair to the choir practices and, even though he couldn't join in, I knew he was enjoying it. It was his song. He was still part of the choir. Elsie and I sang the first verse, then everyone joined in.

Our first crowdfunding concert was booked to take place at the town hall. It was a warm summer evening, and there were lots of tourists in town, eating ice creams and fish and chips. There was even a queue outside the hall waiting for us to start, but Alan Jenkins arrived and cancelled the concert at the last minute saying there had been a water leak in the hall and it was a health and safety issue.

"Nonsense," Jim said. "There's no water leak. He's just angry that we're trying to save the fields he wants to buy."

"What will we do?" said Elsie's dad. "People are here to listen."

"Let's go to the harbour and sing," I said. "We can give out our leaflets there too."

And so we all headed to the harbour – the choir, with Grandad in his wheelchair, and all the people coming to listen. Lots of other people began to come around too. Mum handed out our crowdfunding leaflets, and we began to sing.

There were loads of people there to listen to the choir. We sang so many songs as the sun went down. But when we sang Grandad's song, the "Swan Song", people joined in with the chorus.

The song filled the night and flowed over the marsh and out to sea. I couldn't help asking myself if it would reach the other side of the world.

Chapter 18

Grandad's song did reach the other side of the world.

The next morning Elsie and her dad stopped by.

"Have you heard?" said Elsie.

"What?" I said.

"Open up your computer and see," she said.

I sat down at the kitchen table with them and Mum and Grandad, and switched on the computer to look at the crowdfunding page. I blinked and blinked again.

There had been lots of donations. Some people had given five pounds, and some had given over a hundred pounds. We were on our way to reach our target. Another donation came in as we were watching.

"This isn't a joke, is it?" I said.

Mum shook her head in disbelief, and Grandad banged his hand on the table.

"Maybe there's a real chance that we'll be able to buy the Swan Fields," I said.

Elsie's dad was grinning. "I know. People put it on social media last night, and it went viral. We've had money coming in from all over the world."

"I never knew people loved swans so much," I said.

Elsie's dad smiled. "It's not just the swans. Your grandad's gone viral. Everyone loves a love story. People see it as a love song to his Eve and to the wild."

I turned to Grandad and could see tears falling down his face.

"Grandad!" I said.

But Grandad reached out to type on the computer. **Thank you**, he wrote. **Thank you**.

*

Grandad was different after that. He worked hard with the speech therapist. The speech therapist said he wouldn't be able to sing again, but Grandad still came to every choir practice.

The money kept coming in, but we still didn't have enough to buy Maggie Williams' farm. Then one day Maggie Williams' son turned up at Grandad's house. He had heard about the crowdfunder. He said his mother had loved the swans too. So he said he would sell the Swan Fields to us and the people of the town so that the swans could always find a home here.

And so the Swan Fields were saved. And it wasn't just swans that needed the Swan Fields. There were so many other birds. We saw red kites, water rails and grey wagtails. We had saved a piece of the wild.

The bright greens of early summer turned into the mellow yellows and browns of late August. I often pushed Grandad in the wheelchair to the Swan Fields, where he practised walking along the tracks. Some

evenings there was the chill of autumn in the air and a north breeze.

One evening Grandad sat next to me and typed out one word.

Sorry.

"Sorry for what?" I asked.

I was wrong when I said I lost everything, wrote Grandad. **I have you and your mum. And you are everything to me**.

"It's OK, Grandad," I said.

I needed to say it, typed Grandad. **I didn't want it to be too late to say sorry**.

I just stared at the words. "Sometimes it *is* too late to say sorry," I said. I was remembering something I'd done.

? wrote Grandad.

"I punched Asim," I said. "He was my best friend. My only friend."

Why? wrote Grandad.

I put my head in my hands – I didn't want Grandad to see how bad I felt. "In all the time I was at that school, no one asked me how I felt. Teachers got mad at me, and other pupils cheered me on when I was rude. Asim was the only person who saw how much I was hurting. He was the only one who asked how I felt. I remember he said he didn't like seeing me so sad and said he wanted to help."

So you punched him? wrote Grandad.

I nodded. "I hated him because he cared about me and he saw how low I'd got. I hated myself."

It's not too late to say sorry, wrote Grandad. **Write to him now**.

"What shall I say?"

Exactly what you said to me, wrote Grandad.

*

And I did write a letter. Not a text or an email. I wrote a proper letter in pen on paper, and I sent it all the way across the hills and mountains to the city.

I said sorry.

And I meant it.

I really meant it.

I said sorry to Asim.

Chapter 19

So here I am, waiting for my angel to return.

A whole year has passed, and so much has changed.

I've changed.

Asim wrote back, and he and his mum are going to come and visit us in the Christmas holidays. I can't wait to see him again. I think we'll always be friends, him and me.

I did try school. I went for the first week of a new term at Elsie's school, but it's just not for me. I felt everything crowding in again. I

hated being told what to wear, what to think, what to learn. Mum could see I was unhappy too. She said she'd help home-school me. She's got a new job at a firm in town, and she says I can have a laptop for Christmas to help with my lessons. She's also seeing a lot of Elsie's dad, which is weird but in a good way.

Life is different now. Better.

Much better.

I feel as if I got lost and have now found myself again. I've found the me I like.

I couldn't have done it without my swan.

I know she saved me.

And so here I am again on a chilly October evening. It's the first time Grandad and I have been out on the *Nerys-Jane* since he had his stroke. Grandad is wrapped in blankets,

and I'm steering us up-river on the incoming tide. There is a breeze coming from the north, and the sun is setting, turning the big watery marsh to gold. We pass the houses until we are beside the Swan Fields. I drop the anchor and turn into the tide, the water flowing past us.

We wait and watch the sky turning the fiery colours of sunset.

And then we see a line of birds high, high in the sky, coming from the north. They form a V-shape, one bird at the front, leading the way. Their long necks are stretched out, their wings beating against the thin air. The whooper swans are returning to the Swan Fields as they have done for thousands of years.

And soon they are above us. Their cries and beating wings fill the air with noise. They come in to land on the water around us, their feet stretched out and sliding on the water.

"They're back, Grandad," I yell. "They're back."

Grandad is grinning a big lopsided grin.

And then I see her.

She is the last to come in to land. She flies in a circle with her white wings outspread.

Angel wings.

She sees me, and I see her too.

My swan.

My angel.

She came home.

She came back home.

To me.

Our books are tested
for children and young people by
children and young people.

Thanks to everyone who consulted on
a manuscript for their time and effort in
helping us to make our books better
for our readers.